BRODY THOMPSON
TEXAS RANGER

By Stephen Perez

ISBN: 978-1-965679-92-0 (sc)
ISBN: 978-1-965679-93-7 (e)

Rev. date: 02/20/2025

This book is dedicated to my
two reasons for living.
My two grandsons.

Logan James Perez

&

Jackson Alexander Perez

He starts out chasing bank robbers and ends up with an unanticipated, but welcome love...

He had been in the saddle for days when he came upon the cabin. Brody Thompson wasn't much to look at. He was about 6 feet tall, thin, and wiry, but he was a Texas Ranger, and he was good with a gun. Looking around, he climbed down off the saddle. The cabin looked well-kept, even though there was no sign that anyone or anything had been around recently. Brody was feeling a little uneasy-he had been chasing the O'quin brothers for a few days now and he could feel that he was getting closer. They were two Irish brothers that had been brought in by the railroad to build the tracks. They had gone off and rolled a bank in Abilene.

He looked around a bit. There was a cabin, a barn with a corral, and a few other small buildings. The cabin sat on a small knoll, and it was easy to see all around it. It was late in the day, so he decided he would stay the night.

After he got his horse put away, he went into the cabin to see what kind of shape it was in. He was again surprised at how tidy it was. He looked in the cupboard and found a can of beans and some dried jerky. With some water from his canteen, he made a cup of coffee and sat down to eat.

After supper, he went outside to inspect the other buildings. One was an outhouse and the two others held tack and horse supplies. He was starting to feel the weight of the day, so he decided to call it a night. As the sun was going down, he checked on things once more before going inside to go to bed. He was not used to sleeping on a bed but before he knew it, he was asleep.

He woke up to the crowing of a rooster. In a split second, he was up with his gun in his hand. He did not remember seeing any chickens or roosters the night before. He went outside to a bright, sunny day and sure enough, there was a yard full of chickens and a rooster. He figured they must have been off chasing bugs.

He went back inside and sat down at the table to think for a while. He got up and started to tidy up the place. When he was done, he wrote a note and left it on the table with a silver dollar. He went outside and checked on things one more time. He got his horse and belongings together and headed out.

He had been riding for a while when he came into the town of Gonzales. It was a small, but friendly town. He knew a United States Marshal that had an office there. Roy Perkins was a short, stocky man. He and Brody had been friends for about ten years and Roy had been a lawman as far back as Brody could remember. He went straight to the jailhouse to check in. He walked in a greeted Roy, "Hey, how have you been, you old coot?"

"Oh, I've been better." answered Roy. "I got a telegram from the sheriff in Abilene that said you'd be coming through. It said I should team up with you." "How do you feel about that?" asked Brody. "I'm thinking they're headed south to Mexico," he said. "That would be my guess, too." answered Roy. "I'll need a day to get organized, but it will be nice to ride with you again."

Early the next day, Roy got all his things together, kissed his wife Emma goodbye, and went to meet Brody. Brody knew Roy's wife, too. He had been best man at Roy and Emma's wedding. The two men got their horses from the stable, jumped up into their saddles, and off they went. They talked as they rode, catching up on old times. Brody filled Roy in on the situation. Brody said, "Now Roy, these are a couple of bad hombres. So, be careful and keep your wits about you." "You don't have to tell me anything," commented Roy. "You don't get to be a lawman this long without knowing about being careful."

As they rode, they could see smoke off in the distance. They picked up the pace to a trot. When they got closer, they could see a few wagons overturned and bodies of settlers and Indians strewn all around. "Looks like the Comanches hit a small band of settlers," said Brody. "Yeah, looks like it," added Roy. "Well, let's at least bury the women," he said.

After they finished, they got a drink of water. Brody said, "We better get moving, we've lost a lot of time." As they got in their saddles, they heard a noise from somewhere in the bushes nearby. They got back down off their horses, with guns drawn. As they neared the bushes, they were surprised to find a little girl. "We won't hurt you," said Brody. "We're lawmen." The little girl, about six years old, slowly came out of the bushes. She was crying and the men could tell she was scared and nervous. "What's your name, little girl'?" asked Brody. "My name is Sarah," she said. "My mother told me to hide here when the Indians came." "How long ago did they come?" asked Roy. The little girl said, "I don't know how long ago, but it's been a while." "We are going to have to take her with us," said Roy. "We can't just leave her out here by herself."

Brody gave Roy an impatient look. "I guess you're right," said Brody. "But we have lost a lot of time already." Roy put her in the saddle with him. He seemed to be the more caring of the two, and they headed out. "We will drop her off at the next town," said Brody. As they rode into a little stagecoach stop, just outside of a little town called Cuero, they decided they would leave the little girl there.

As they rode up to a house, an elderly man came out to greet them. "Howdy! Name's Tom. Tom Johnston. I'm the caretaker of this place," he said. Roy and Brody got off their horses and Roy gently got the little girl down and put her on the ground next to him. "You the only one here?" asked Brody. "No," said Tom. "I have my daughter here with me. She's inside preparing supper for the folks on the next stage that's due here in the next hour."

"Where's the stage headed?" asked Brody. "It's headed to Austin. Why?" asked Tom. "We found this little girl at a camp that was attacked by Indians. She was the only survivor," said Brody. Sarah heard them say this, about where the stage was going, and she jumped up and spoke out. "I overheard my mother and father talking about someone living in Austin! I think they said it was my father's sister." "Good, good." said Brody. "That is where we will send you. What is your last name, Sarah?" asked Brody. "Anderson," she replied. "My last name is Anderson." Brody cut in and asked Tom, "You said that your daughter was here with you?" "That's right." Tom said. "Do you think that she would be willing to escort Sarah to Austin to find her aunt?" asked Brody. "You will have to ask her, but I don't see a problem with that," Tom said. They all went inside the station to talk to Tom's daughter.

Once inside, they saw a short, slender girl, preparing something on the stove. "Mary, these men are lawmen, and they want to talk to you," said Tom. "I don't know if this is going to work," said Brody, "She's just a kid herself!" Tom turned, looking at both men, and said, "She might not look like much, but she's tough as nails. I would put her up against any man." "How old are you?" Brody asked her. "I'm seventeen, but I will be eighteen next week." Mary said. "Do you think you could handle taking this little girl to Austin to find her aunt?" asked Brody. "Of course, I would pay you," he added. Mary looked a little hesitant when he asked her. "I'm not sure if I can do that," she said. "Why not?" asked Brody. "My father has a lot to do around here. I don't want to leave him here with all the work. "Now, Mary, you go ahead and do this here thing," said Tom. "I will be okay." "Besides, that little girl needs you. So, it's settled," said Brody. "Y'all can head out on the stage tomorrow." "Fine," said Mary. "Are you boys hungry? I'm just finishing up some beef stew." It was late in the day, so Brody decided that they would spend the night there.

While they were eating their supper, a young man came in the door. Brody instantly noticed that he was wearing a badge. Tom went and said hello to him and introduced him to Brody and Roy. "Howdy! Name's Jim. Jim Hawkins. I'm the deputy in Cuero. The sheriff sent me out here to ask if y'all would come into town to see him." "He wants to see us tonight? asked Brody. "Tomorrow morning will be fine if it's okay with y'all," said Jim. "Do you know what it's about," said Roy? Well, I'll just let him tell y'all, said Jim. "We will be in first thing in the morning," said Brody. Maybe he can buy us breakfast, joked Roy. Jim laughed, turned around and left. Brody asked Tom if he knew the sheriff. He wanted to know what kind of man he was. Tom said, "e's young, 25 if he's a day, smart as a pistol. He's only been sheriff a couple of months. Some desperados came into town and killed our old sheriff."

The town thought he might be too young, but nobody else wanted the job. "He's been doing a fair job. No complaints." "Well, I think I'll go outside and smoke a cigarette," said Roy. "Don't y'all want some dessert?" asked Mary. "I made a blueberry pie." "Think I'll pass on that," said Brody. Me too, said Roy. I don't think I could eat another bite. Both men got up and made their way outside. The next day, both men were up at dawn. Since Mary was not up yet, Brody started making some coffee. Both he and Roy were eager to see what the sheriff wanted from them. As both men were sitting at the table drinking their coffee, Mary came in with Sarah right behind her. "Would y'all like some breakfast?" "I can fix y'all something right quick," said Mary. "No, I reckon not," replied Brody. "Coffee will do. Besides, we are anxious to find out what the sheriff wants. We want to see you and Sarah off on the stage, and then we're going to head that way."

An hour went by, and the stage finally showed up. They got Mary and Sarah on the stage, and Brody gave Mary some money. "That should take care of everything," said Brody. "Well, thank you," said Mary, "and I will see that Sarah gets to her aunt." After the stage left, Brody and Roy said their goodbyes and headed out.

Cuero was a small, friendly little town, with all the people just going about their business. As they rode up to the jail, the sheriff came out to greet them. "How y'all boys doing?" asked the sheriff." Oh, we've seen better days," replied Brody. As they got off their horses, the sheriff introduced himself. "Name's Fred Jones," said the sheriff. "My name's Brody, and this here is Roy Perkins," replied Brody. "Well, you boys, come in and let's talk," said Fred. "I was hoping to talk to y'all about a problem I'm having. You being a Texas Ranger and all, Mr. Thompson," said Fred. "What kind of problem are you having that requires a ranger? And the name's Brody," replied Brody.

"Well, there's a big landowner, rancher, by the name of Brad Jennings." "I've heard of him," said Roy. "He owns the Lazy Jay Ranch, doesn't he?" "He's supposed to be pretty big in these parts, ain't he?"" said Roy. "Yeah, he's

the biggest this side of the Colorado," said Fred. "Okay," said Brody. "Back to the problem you said you had." "Well," said" Fred, "the railroad wants to lay tracks through some of his property, and he's giving them hell. He told them that if any of them came on his land, he would bury them." "Why doesn't the government handle this?" replied Brody. "I was just going to head out and go talk to Mr. Perkins, he being a U.S. Marshal and all. But then I heard that y'all might be coming through. That's why I sent word to y'all." "Give us a minute to talk about it," said Brody. Both men stepped outside. This is your jurisdiction," said Brody to Roy.

"Do you think you can handle it by yourself?" "I can, but I would sure feel better if we both went," said Roy. They both stepped back inside and told the sheriff that they would go and talk to Mr. Jennings. "Oh, by the way, I forgot to mention that he has brought in a couple of gunfighters," said Fred. "Sure, he did," replied Brody, and he and Roy just looked at each other. "You boys want some breakfast?" asked Fred." I'm buying. It's the least I can do." "Okay," said Brody, "But you're coming over there with us." The three men ate their breakfast and then headed out. The sheriff had told the deputy to keep an eye on things.

When they had gotten about five miles from the Lazy J Ranch, they came up on some riders. "State your business,"

one rider said. "We are lawmen," said Brody, "coming to talk to Mr. Jennings." "Well, Mr. Jennings don't want to talk to no one, so y'all can just turn around and go back the way y'all came." "Bill," replied Fred, "this is Brody Thompson. He's a Texas Ranger. And the other fella is Roy Perkins. He's a U.S. Marshal." "That don't mean squat to me," said Bill, as he was drawing his gun. Before anyone knew what had happened, all three men lay dead on the ground. "Man," said Fred, "I had heard you were fast with a gun, but I didn't really know how fast till now." "He's probably the fastest gun in Texas," said Roy. As they rode up to the ranch house, a well-dressed pretty, young girl came walking out of the door." I guess you boys are here to talk to my father?" asked the girl.

"Linda, these men are lawmen wanting to talk to your father about the railroad situation," said Fred. "This thing has gotten out of hand." "This is Brody Thompson. He's a Texas Ranger. And the other one is Roy Perkins. He's a U.S. Marshal." "Y'all must be really good to get past our greeting party," replied Linda. Brody spoke out, "We are not here to cause trouble. We would like to handle this peaceful-like." Linda called out to some of the men. "You boys come take care of these horses while I get my father." The three men got off their horses and followed Linda into the house. It was a very well-built ranch house, Brody noticed. As they came in, Mr. Jennings was coming down the stairs. "Father," said Linda, "These men are with the law. They would like to talk to you." "I see their badges," said Mr. Jennings. "You can talk all you want. It's not going to change anything." "Mr. Jennings," said Brody. "My name is Brody Thompson, and this here is Roy Perkins. He's a United States Marshal." "You can call me Brad, but like I said, it ain't going to change anything."

"This is my land, and they ain't gonna take it from me." "Well," said Roy, "How about if we get the railroad people together with you and talk things out? There ain't no harm in that, is there?" "Father," said Linda, "Please listen to what they have to say. I don't want anyone to get hurt." "Okay, fine," said Brad. "You set up a meeting, and I will sit and listen. But if I'm not promising anything." "That's all we ask," said Fred. "Well, I guess we're done here for now," said Brody. They all went outside, where their horses were waiting for them. The three men got on their horses, tipped their hats to Linda, and rode off. As they rode, Roy began talking to Brody. "Hey, partner, you realize this is going to take a while?" "I was just thinking that myself," said Brody.

"I know you wanted to catch those bank robbers, and I have taken a lot of your time," continued Roy. "I don't have any right to ask you to stay and help, but I could really use your help." "I know," said Brody. "Let me think on the situation a bit, and I will get back with you." Riding back into town, the deputy came out to greet them. "Something wrong, Jim?" asked Fred. "Well, while y'all were out there talking, we got a telegram," said Jim. "It appears those two Irish brothers hit another bank, this time in Bandera." "They shot and killed the sheriff and the deputy. I thought Mr. Thompson might want to know that." "Thank you for letting me know," replied Brody. "I'm obliged to ya." Jim just nodded and walked off. "I'm going to have to go over there and see what I can do," said Brody. "I'll go with you," said Roy. Brody started to say something, but Roy cut him off.

"You know it's gonna take these railroad men at least a week to get down here for any meeting." "You're right," said Brody," but I can't promise that this will be handled in that time frame." "Yep," said Roy, "I will just have to play it by ear." It was already midday, and Brody was anxious. "Well, whatever you're going to do, we need to get a move on it," said Brody. "How will I keep you updated on the railroad meeting?" asked Fred. "We will send you telegrams every now and then to check up on things," replied Brody. Brody and Roy packed up their things and headed out for Bandera. It was late when they pulled into Bandera. "There's the Silver Dollar Saloon," said Roy. "We should go in and get a drink, and maybe get some information on the bank job." "That's a good idea,"

said Brody. They got off their horses and headed inside. "What'll it be?" asked the bartender.

"We'll have a beer," said Brody. "We heard y'all had some trouble down here," said Roy. "We had a bank hold up, if that's what you're talking about," said the bartender. "Don't know too much about it. The banker is over at the hotel, if you boys want to talk to him," said the bartender. "I noticed the badges when y'all walked in. The banker is pretty shook up, but he should be able to answer your questions." "Much obliged," said Brody. They paid for the drinks and walked out. They then walked into the hotel. Behind the counter was a tall, lanky man with a handlebar mustache. "You boys need a room?" asked the man. "No," said Brody. "We're here to talk to the bank president about what happened." "Okay," said the man. "He's in room 210, up the stairs, second door down the hall to the right." "Thanks," said Brody. They headed upstairs. They knocked on the door, and a man opened it. Brody introduced them and told the man why they were there. The man went on to introduce himself as Dr. Grant. "Now you boys can talk to him but be gentle. He's been through a lot. His name is Ben Hale," said the doctor. After they got the specifics, they went downstairs and asked the clerk about the livery stable. Brody wanted to head out, but Roy interjected. "Now, Brody, I don't know about you, but I am just plain tuckered out. I think we should get

us a room, get some rest, and then look at the situation in the morning." "I guess you're right," said Brody. "We can't do too much tonight an

Brody was up early. He did not sleep very well, thinking and worrying about the situation he was in. He got up and went downstairs. The hotel was very nice, and it had a little area where you could sit and drink some coffee. He poured him some coffee and sat down to think. As he was sitting there, he could not help but think about Linda. She was beautiful, well-educated, and stirred emotions in him. After a while, he laughed and came back to himself. "I don't have time for this," he thought to himself. He started thinking about the O'Quin brothers and how they had started back north, instead of keeping south the way he had figured. He could not, for the life of him, figure out what they had in mind. It was daybreak when Roy came walking down the stairs. "How long have you been down here?" asked Roy. "For a while," answered Brody.

"Well, what's our next move?" asked Roy. "That's what I've been down here trying to figure out," said Brody. "I just can't figure out what happened. "Why would they start back north?" asked Brody. "Excuse me, senores? said an elderly Mexican man who was sitting within earshot distance to the men. "I could not help but overhear what y'all were talking about," said the man. "My name is Pedro

Garcia, and I know of the man you're talking about. I was in the saloon the night they came in, before they robbed the bank. I sit close to them, and I hear them making the plans." "The one man does not want to rob the bank, but the other one says that they need the money to get home. "That's why they said that they needed the money- to get home?" asked Brody. "Si," said Pedro. "They need to get to a town called Galveston to get on a boat. "They must be getting home sick," said Roy. "Yeah," replied Brody. "Sounds like it."

They thanked the man, got up, and walked out. "We need to send a telegram to Fred," said Brody. "Let him know what's going on." "This might take a little longer than I thought," said Brody. "You gonna stick with me, Roy?" "I've come this far," said Roy. "I reckon I'll stick it out if it's okay with you." "Well, we better get a move on it," said Brody. "We've got a long ride ahead of us." They headed to the library stable to get their horses. As they were crossing the street, some men came riding into town. "Y'all must be Thompson and Perkins?" said one man. "That would be us," said Brody. "Who's asking?" "Mr. Jennings wants y'all back at the ranch, and we don't keep Mr. Jennings waiting," said the man. "I'm sorry y'all made this trip for nothing," said Brody. "But we have other business to take care of, and we're headed to Galveston." The man drew

his pistol and said, "I don't think you heard me right. I said we don't keep Mr. Jennings waiting."

Before he could pull the trigger, he and two others lay dead in the street. "Tell Mr. Jennings we will be getting there some time," said Brody. "We are chasing some bank robbers, and a ranger always gets his man." The other riders just turned and rode away. "We might ought to get some provisions," said Brody. "I want to hit the road hard. I want to get these men so we can get back and deal with Mr. Jennings." "I'm with you," said Roy. After they sent the telegram and got some supplies, they hit the road. They had been riding for a while when they came upon a little town called Sandy Fork. It wasn't much, just a few little buildings. Roy noticed the saloon. "I sure could use a drink right about now. Wash off some of that trail dust." "Okay," said Brody, "but we're going to ride on through the night." They stopped in front of the saloon and got off and went in. "A couple of beers," said Brody, "and a bottle" interjected Roy. They sat down at a table and started talking about everything that had happened. There were some men playing cards at another table. They yelled out to the pair. "Care for a game of cards?" Brody shook his head no, but Roy was feeling lucky. "Don't mind if I do," said Roy. "What are we playing?" asked Roy as he pulled up a chair. One man called out, "seven card draw, aces high." "Well, deal me in," said Roy. Brody just sat at the table thinking about

things. A saloon girl came over and asked Brody to buy her a drink. "Pull up a chair," said Brody, as he motioned to the bartender. "My name's Martha," said the girl. "What brings y'all to Sandy Fork? We don't get too many visitors." "We're just passing through," answered Brody. "Where are y'all headed?" asked Martha. "We have business in Galveston," answered Brody. "That's a long way off," said Martha. Before Brody could say anything, the card game got a little rowdy. He overheard Roy accusing one of the other players of cheating

The accused man had not taken it lightly. He reached for his gun, but Brody already had his gun out. "I wouldn't do that if I were you," said Brody. Instead, the man turned the table over and jumped at Roy. Roy fell back but quickly recovered and grabbed the man, flipping him over. Before the man could get up, Roy was on top of him. He had grabbed him by the collar, stood him up, and hit him as hard as he could. The man fell back, and he was out. The other men sat there in disbelief. Roy walked over to the man on the floor and checked his sleeves. Sure enough, the man had a few cards stuck up inside his sleeves. One of the other men spoke out, "Would you lookie there?" "We thought he was getting a little too lucky." Brody got up from the table, said goodbye to Martha, and motioned to Roy. "We better get out of here before he comes to." "He's not gonna be happy." "There's no law here!" yelled

Martha. "We are the law!" cried Brody. They walked out, got on their horses, and left. They rode on through the night. It was early morning. The sun was just coming up when they saw the lights of another little town. "It sure would be nice to get some breakfast," said Roy. "I'm so hungry. The past couple of hours, I've been thinking of eating my horse

"Yeah," answered Brody. "I guess I could throw down some vittles. I would also like to know where we are." They saw a building that had a sign on it that read, *Mama Roses.* "That looks like it might be a fine establishment," said Roy. "Yeah, well, let's get at it," said Brody. They got off their horses and went inside. The first thing Brody smelled was the coffee. "It sure smells good in here," said Brody. "You boys take a seat where you want," yelled an older-looking lady. "I'll be right with y'all." They picked out a table close to a window. This way, we can kind of keep an eye on things happening outside," said Brody. "That's smart," said Roy. Finally, the older lady came over to them. "My name is Rose. I own this place. Now, how can I help y'all?" "Well, first thing, you can bring us some of that good smelling coffee," said Brody. "We have some questions to ask when you come back with the coffee," said Brody. "I'll be right back with the coffee and hopefully some answers," said the lady. She was gone for about 10 minutes. When she came back, she had two

cups and a pot of coffee. "Sorry," said the lady, "I had to make a fresh pot." She turned to Brody. "You had some questions for me?" asked the lady. "Yeah," said Brody. "Can you tell us where we are?" "You're in Pipe Creek," answered the lady.

"Can you tell us how far it is to Galveston?" asked Brody. "It's still at least a couple of days ride away." "That's a pretty good-sized town," said Rose. "I've heard they do a lot of business there, and a lot of shady happenings as well." "Y'all got business there?" asked Rose. "We're lawmen after a couple of bank robbers," answered Brody. "You didn't happen to see a couple of strangers come through any time before us, did you?" asked Brody. "Couldn't have been too long ago. A day, maybe," said Roy. "No, can't say as I have," said Rose, "but that doesn't really mean anything. I don't see everyone that comes through, unless they come in here. Y'all gonna want some breakfast? If not, I have work to do," said Rose. Roy was hungry, so they placed their order and waited. While they were waiting, a young man came in and looked around. He saw the two men sitting there and walked over to them. "Would y'all happen to be Thompson and Perkins?" asked the man. "Yes, it would," replied Brody. "Who's asking?" "I work at the telegraph office. The clerk saw y'all ride in and asked me to find out if it was y'all. Said if it *was* y'all, to tell y'all that he had a telegram for

you," said the man. "Much obliged," said Brody. "We will be over as soon as we finish our breakfast." With that, the man turned around and left.

After they had finished, Brody called Rose over. "Can you tell us whereabouts that telegraph office is?" asked Brody. "It's across the street on the other side of town," answered Rose. They got their hats, left some money on the table, and left. As they were crossing the street, a man with a badge walked up to them. "Howdy. My name's Walt," said the man. "I'm the sheriff here in this little town, and I just want to know who comes and goes through here." "Howdy, Sheriff," said Brody. "I'm Texas Ranger Brody Thompson, and this is U.S. Marshal Roy Perkins. We are just passing through on our way to Galveston. We stopped for some breakfast, and we were told we had a telegram waiting for us. That's where we're headed now, and after that, we will be riding out." "Y'all let me know if I can be of any help," said the sheriff. "Say, are y'all the two that are after the boys that robbed the bank in Bandera?" "That would be correct," answered Brody. "Well, y'all be careful, and good luck," said the sheriff as he walked away.

They walked on down the street to the telegraph office. Coming up to the building, they opened the door and walked in. "Howdy," said the man. "I'm the head clerk here. We got this telegram in late last night. I saw you

boys ride into town and figured this telegram was for you." "Much obliged," said Brody. The man handed the telegram over to Brody, and he quickly opened it and began to read the telegram:

"L to Mr. Brody Thompson. Stop. The railroad men cannot come down for about a month. Stop. We'*ll keep you advised. Stop. Sheriff Fred Jones."*

"Well, what's it say?" asked Roy. "Meeting with the railroad won't be for another month," answered Brody. "Well, that's good. Gives us a little more time with this situation," answered Roy. They thanked the clerk and walked out. Once outside, Brody stopped to think about what could possibly happen next.

"What exactly are you thinking?" asked Roy. "I'm trying to figure out what to do next," answered Brody. "For the first time in my life, I'm stumped. Let's go have a beer while I decide what to do," said Brody. They walked into the saloon and sat down at a table. They motioned to the bartender for some beer. "I don't like it, Roy," said Brody. "Don't like what?" asked Roy. "Never in my life have I had a feeling of not knowing what to do next," said Brody. "Well, it'll come to you," said Roy. "Always does." Before they knew it, it was late afternoon and they had gone through a few beers. "You know what?" said Brody. "You got a plan?" said

Roy. "I think I'm going to send a telegram to the sheriff in Galveston, letting him know that we're coming and what we're doing," said Brody. "Good idea, "said Roy. "That way he will know and be on the lookout for us."

They went back to the telegraph office so Brody could send the telegram. Walking out of the building, Brody felt a little better. Brody, talking to Roy, says, "We should be there within the next few days. Being so late, I think we should get a room and get a good night's rest and head out first light." "Sounds like a plan," answered Roy. They headed to the hotel, got a room, and called it a night. They were both up before the sun. They headed out to the livery stables to check on their horses.

The man at the stable had some bad news for Brody. "Is that Mustang yours?" asked the man. "Yes, it is," answered Brody. "He's a beautiful horse, but he has a bum leg," said the man. "I don't think he's going to be of any use to you right now. He'll need at least a couple of days' rest to get back to himself." "I need him right now," said Brody. "I have two others you can pick from," said the man. "Another Mustang or an Appaloosa you can use." "Well, I'm kind of partial to Mustangs," said Brody. "I'm going to take him for now, but I'll be back for Sam when I'm done. I've had him since he was a colt." They both got on their saddles and took off. They had been riding for a few miles when Roy began a conversation with Brody that he had wanted to talk to him about but kept putting it off. "Listen, Brody," started Roy. "I need you to make me a promise." "What is it?" asked Brody. "You know that I would do anything for you." "Well, this is hard for me to say, but I need you to understand," said Roy. "Okay," said Brody. "You know Emma means the world to me," started Roy. "What are you saying?" interjected Brody. "Would you just shut up and listen? I have thought about this a lot," said Roy. "We are going into a real dangerous situation, and no one knows what will happen. If, and this is a big if, something was to happen to me, I need to know in my heart that Emma will be taken good care of. I know that she has a place in your heart. That's why I chose you to be my best man. I need you to promise me that if something happens to me, that you will take Emma as your wife and take care of her." "Nothing's going to happen to you. You're as tough as nails," said Brody. "Please promise me, Brody," said Roy. "Okay," said Brody. "I promise that if something happens to you, but nothing will, I will take care of Emma."

"Does that make you happy?" Brody asked. "Yes, it does, and it takes a big load off my mind," said Roy. "Thank you. Now we can get back to business at hand," said Brody. They talked as they rode, making plans as to how things might go down. They were so preoccupied with their task that they did not realize that they had come into another little town. When they came to a stop, they were in front of a saloon. "Great," said Brody. "Let's have a beer and talk to someone." Before they went in, Brody told Roy to take off his badge, and he did the same. "Why?" asked Roy. "Because from here on out, I don't want anyone to know who we are or that we are lawmen," commented Brody. "I don't understand," said Roy, "but okay." "Well," said Brody, "the plan that I have come up with in my head requires total anonymity. I want to take them by surprise if possible."

"Are you going to share that plan with me," questioned Roy. "That's why I wanted to stop in here and fill you in on it," said Brody. "A couple of beers," yelled Brody to the bartender. When the bartender came over with the beers, Brody asked him where they were and how far it was to Galveston. "Well," said the bartender, "you're in the town of Hitchcock, and you could be in Galveston by tonight." "Thanks," said Brody. Brody started filling Roy in on his plan. "I sent that telegram to the sheriff in Galveston," said Brody. "I told him what I'm about to tell you. When we get to Galveston, we will check in with the sheriff. They will have a manifest of all the people boarding the ship. When we see the names of the O'Quin brothers on the manifest, we will go down and wait with the ship's captain. The captain will be checking the names of people as they board the ship."

"When the brothers come up, we will take them right there, hopefully it will go down peacefully." "Well, it sounds like a pretty good plan," said Roy. "I just hope nothing goes wrong." "Well,"" said Brody, "let's get out of here. I'm ready to get this done." They drank their beers, went out, got on their horses and rode off. It was late when they got to Galveston. It was a good-sized town, Brody noticed. Bigger than he had imagined. It took them a little while to locate the sheriff's office. They got off their horses and walked into the sheriff's office. The building was big and as they walked in, they were greeted by a man behind a large counter. "May I help you?" asked the man. "We're here to see the sheriff," said Brody. "Is the sheriff expecting you?" inquired the man. "We sent him a telegram a couple of days ago letting him know what we're doing," said Brody. "Oh, okay," said the man. "Y'all must be Thompson and Perkins. The sheriff asked me to be on the lookout for y'all. If y'all want to come this way, I will take y'all to the sheriff." He led them down a long hallway and stopped in front of a door with a name on it. He knocked, and a voice from inside invited them to come in. The man opened the door and went in, followed by Brody and Roy. "These are the men you've been waiting for," exclaimed the man. "Thank you. That will be all," said the sheriff. "I'm Sheriff Doug Smith, and y'all must be Ranger Thompson and Marshal Perkins," remarked the sheriff. "This is a bigger town than

I imagined," said Brody. "You have a big operation here. How many men do you have under you?" questions Brody. "There are ten deputies and four constables," answered the sheriff. "We stay pretty busy. In the telegram, you said there would be two men wanting to board a ship?" inquired the sheriff. "Yes," said Brody. They are two Irish brothers, and they were overheard making plans to board a ship to go home." "Well, there won't be any ships coming or going till tomorrow night," said the sheriff. "There won't be any ships coming or going till tomorrow night," said the sheriff. "I won't even have the manifest till tomorrow morning, sometime."

"Y'all can get you a room at the hotel around the corner tonight and come back in the morning. And we will make our plans," said Doug. The two men got up and walked out. They stopped at the front desk to inquire about the hotel. "The sheriff said there was a hotel around the corner?" asked Brody. "Yes," said the man. "That would be the Majestic Hotel. Just walk out the front door here, take a left, go down to the corner, and you will see it across the street." "Where is the stable to keep our horses?" inquired Brody. "Don't worry about that," answered the man. "They will be taken care of for you." "Thank you," said Brody. The two men went outside, got some saddlebags from their horses, and headed to the hotel.

They saw the sign for the Majestic Hotel. As they walked in, they were baffled. They asked the clerk if they were in the right place. "If you're looking for the Majestic," queried the clerk, "then you're in the right place." "We didn't know if this was a hotel or a saloon," said Roy.

"Did you boys want a room?" inquired the clerk. They each got a room. "I think we should have a drink before we turn in for the night," said Roy. "All right" said Brody, "but just one." They walked into a big room and sat down at a table. A man walked up to them and asked what they wanted to drink. They put in their order and the man walked away. When the man came back with the beers, Roy asked him a question. "What's going on through that door?" "That's a gambling room," said the man. "There are a couple of card tables and some other gambling games." "Is that right?" asked Roy. "Now, Roy," said Brody, "you stay out of there. You remember what happened in Sandy Fork. We don't have time for all that nonsense. We had better get to our rooms. Tomorrow is going to be a busy day." "Fine," said Roy. They finished their beers and went on up to their rooms. It was early morning and Brody was up. He still could not sleep very well. Something kept nagging at him. He kept thinking about the promise that Roy had asked him to keep. He went downstairs to the lobby to see if he could get some coffee. To his surprise, Roy was already down there, sitting and drinking a cup of coffee. "Fancy seeing you down here already," said Brody. "I couldn't sleep. I had too much on my mind," answered Roy. "I know what you mean," said Brody. "Me too." They both sat there in silence, drinking their coffee. Finally, Brody said, "We better get on down and see the sheriff." They both got up and went to see the man at the counter. "Thompson and Perkins checking out," said Brody. "Everything is taken care of," said the man. They got their belongings and left. As they were coming up to the sheriff's office, the sheriff was coming out. "Good morning, sheriff," said Brody. "Good morning," said Doug. "Have you boys had breakfast yet?" the sheriff asked. "No," said Brody. "I don't think I could eat anything right now." "Well, I sure can," said Doug. "You boys can tag along if you want. It's too early for anything anyway." So, Brody and Roy followed the sheriff down the road. They all went into a shack of a building. "This place might not look like much," said the sheriff, "but they have the best food in town." They sat down at a table in a back room. "I know y'all want to keep this as hush-hush as possible. That's why I chose this place." "Well, we might as well get something to eat, then, "said Brody.

The three men sat there eating their breakfast and talking for a good while. "Well, I guess we should get down to the office and see what's going on," said the sheriff. They got their hats, got up, and walked out. As they walked, the sheriff was telling Brody and Roy a little about the town.

They got to the door of the sheriff's office and walked in. "You boys go on back to my office if you remember where that is?" asked the sheriff, "I'll go talk to the clerk, see if he's heard anything." "I remember," said Brody. "We will wait for you there." A few minutes later, the sheriff walked into the office with a sheet of paper. "This is the manifest for the Derby," said the sheriff. "That's the ship your boys are waiting for. Their names are on there, the O'Quin brothers, Connor and Liam." "It's not quite here yet. It's set to dock right after noon and depart at 5 p.m. this afternoon. It's a cargo ship, so there won't be very many passengers," added the sheriff. "Have you talked to the captain?" asked Brody.

"Yes, I talked to him last night," said the sheriff. "He's expecting y'all, and I told him y'all would have the manifest with you. It's the only copy." It was mid-morning, so they just sat there talking and anxiously waiting. The sheriff finally told Brody and Roy that they could go down and get with the captain of the ship. To Brody, it had seemed like an eternity, and he was eager to go. "I'll be down there later, myself," said the sheriff. "Remember," said Brody, "no badges." "I'll remember," said the sheriff. The two men got up, said their goodbyes, and left. It was a good way to the dock, so the sheriff had arranged for a ride for the men. They were not accustomed to riding in a buggy, so they were a bit apprehensive. "Well, I guess it's either this or walk," said Roy. Brody agreed, and they got in. When they got to the docks, they were already loading the ship with cargo. There was a man in a uniform giving out orders, so Brody took him to be the captain. They walked up to him and introduced themselves. "Yes," said the captain. "The sheriff told me to be expecting y'all." "There will only be about 20 people going on this trip," said the captain. "I will have them in a line and read their names before they can board." "As the two brothers come up, y'all can do whatever it is that y'all are going to do." "Sounds simple enough," said Brody. The passengers started showing up a little later, and the captain told them to form a line. It was getting close to 4:30, so the captain started calling names out for people to board. There was no sign of the two brothers, and Brody started to get worried. As the captain got to the end of the list, the two brothers came walking up. "Good," thought, Brody. "They don't seem like they expect anything out of the ordinary." He was also pleased because they looked to be unarmed. The captain called out their names. "Connor and Liam O'Quin?" The two men started walking toward them.

As they did, Brody and Roy approached them. "You boys are under arrest," said Brody as he pulled his gun out. This action startled the two men and they started to fall back. As they fell back, Connor, the older of the two, pulled a gun out of his shirt and managed to fire once. Brody fired and killed them both instantly. The O'Quin brothers lay dead.

And to Brody's surprise, he noticed that Roy had also been shot.

The sheriff, who had just walked up, sent for a doctor. But Brody knew that it was too late. As Brody sat there with Roy's head on his lap, he said, "As fast as I am, I was not fast enough to save the life of my friend and partner. I'm sorry," said Brody. "It's okay," said Roy, "just don't forget your promise," he whispered as he took his last breath.

Two weeks later, Emma steps out of her front door and sees Brody riding up. She starts to smile and then notices that Brody has Roy's unsaddled horse next to him, and without a word she falls to her knees, sobbing.

Brody Thompson
Texas Ranger

By Stephen Perez

Part Two: Brody's Promise

Morning came with Brody sleeping in the barn. Although he had not slept a wink, he kept turning what had happened over and over in his head. Any way that he looked at it, he felt responsible for the death of his friend. He was thinking so hard on the matter that he had not heard Emma walk in.

"How did you sleep?" asked Emma.

"I didn't," answered Brody.

"I still wish you had slept in the house," said Emma. "Well, breakfast is already on the table, so come on in and eat. I want to talk to you anyway."

As they walked to the house, Brody was thinking about what he would say to Emma. They walked into the house, and Emma told Brody to sit at the table. Breakfast was already laid out, just as she had said. She told him that they would eat first in silence and then talk afterward. When breakfast was over, they both still sat there in silence, just looking at each other.

Emma started the conversation by asking Brody, "What happened?"

Brody took a deep breath and began to explain, "We got caught up with two brothers over in Galveston, and it was supposed to be quick and easy. We were standing there with the captain of the ship as the two brothers walked toward us. I told them that they were under arrest, and I hadn't noticed any weapons on them, so I thought it would be easy. But, when we did this, they started falling back, and Connor, the older of the two, pulled a gun out of his shirt and fired once. As he did that, I pulled my own gun and fired twice. I killed both of them.

"When I finally stood up, I noticed Roy was lying on the ground, and I knew then that he had been hit. The sheriff left to get the doctor, but it was too late. I knelt down and put Roy's head on my lap. Emma, he was still alive at this point, and I told him that I was sorry. But he said that it was not my fault, and as he was taking his last breaths, he told me not to forget about the promise I had made to him."

"And what promise was that?" asked Emma.

"Well, that is something that we seriously need to discuss," answered Brody. "Before you get all bent out of shape, just listen to what I have to say all the way to the end. Will you promise not to say anything until I am done saying what I have to say?"

"I promise, I guess," answered Emma.

"First off, you know how I feel about you," said Brody. "With that being said, Roy was real serious about what we talked about, and he was really worried about what would happen to you if something were to happen to him. That's why he made me promise to take you as my wife and take care of you."

Emma opened her mouth as if to say something, but Brody reminded her of the promise to listen.

Brody went on, "I would be honored to take you as my wife, but I know how independent, hard-headed, and stubborn you are. I have been thinking about this a lot, and if you're not willing, I don't have to marry you to take care of you. I can just be around and look in on you now and then, and I would still be keeping my promise to Roy. But, if you're up for it after a while has passed, and if you feel like it, then we could get hitched. What do you think?"

"Can I speak now?" asked Emma.

Brody nodded.

"I really loved my Roy, so I cannot just turn that switch off and on. It will take me some time to do my grieving.

You also know how I feel about you. I don't think I need anyone to take care of me. However, I know Roy thought highly of you, and you of him. I'll think about this idea for the future, but I think we can go on with your plan for now. I have chores to do, but we will talk again later."

Emma got up and headed outside, while Brody sat there, dumbfounded, at the table.

It seemed to Brody like the day dragged on forever. Evening finally came, and they both sat down again at the table, this time for supper. Brody started the conversation. "Tomorrow, I must go down south for a bit. A big landowner is having trouble with the railroad, and I need to go down there and help work things out. That will give you time to think on things. I don't know how long I will be gone, but I will be back."

"OK," said Emma. "But you will sleep in that extra room. I fixed it up for you, and I won't hear another word on it."

"Fine," said Brody. "I'm going outside to smoke a cigarette and check on things before I turn in for the night."

The next morning, while Brody was getting ready to leave, he heard a horse approaching and went outside to see who it was. It was a man from town.

"Are you Brody Thompson?" asked the man.

"That's right," said Brody.

"I have a telegram for you," the man said. "It came in late last night."

The man handed the telegram to Brody and left.

About that time, Emma came walking into the house and inquired about the man who had just left. Brody told her about the telegram.

"Well, what does it say?" asked Emma.

"I haven't even read it yet," remarked Brody.

After reading the telegram, Brody told Emma the contents. "They are sending in another marshal for the district," said Brody. "They know about Mr. Jennings and the railroad. They want me to wait for him and bring him up to speed on the situation."

"When will he be here?" asked Emma.

"Won't be for another two weeks or so, and they want me to keep things calm around here until he gets here."

"Well, that's good," said Emma. "Maybe that will give us time to get used to each other."

"I'm going into town," said Brody. "I reckon I need to see about looking for a deputy."

Brody went out to get his horse saddled. He left without saying anything else to Emma. When he got to the jailhouse, he started looking through some papers that were on the desk. He did not know the town or the townspeople here very well. He thought to himself, "*This is going to be some kind of job!*"

He decided to go to the saloon to have a beer and look things over. While he was there, a fight broke out. One of the men had accused the other of trying to take his saloon girl away from him. They started fist fighting. Brody broke up the fight and told them they were under arrest. As he started taking one of them to jail, the other man drew his gun and was going to shoot Brody. But a young man who was standing at the bar saw the man draw his gun to shoot Brody. The young man drew his gun and fired a shot at the man who was targeting Brody. The man instantly fell dead.

Brody thanked the man and asked him to go to the jail with him. He wanted to talk with him.

"I must be getting old," said Brody. "In my younger days, I wouldn't have let him get the drop on me like that."

"Well, these things happen," said the young man.

"I'm sorry," said Brody. "What did you say your name was?"

"My name's Walt. Walt Harris," said the young man.

"I like your intuitive nature and your fast hand," stated Brody. "I'm looking for a deputy to help out for a couple of weeks. Pay is $5 a week if you're interested. I say for a couple of weeks because they're sending in a new U.S. Marshal. It will be up to him if he wants to keep you on."

"I've always been interested in the law," answered Walt. "I guess I could give it a try. If it works out, I wouldn't mind settling down here."

Brody swore him in and spent the rest of the afternoon filling him in on things that had happened and things that were possibly about to happen.

"I'm sorry about your partner, but it sounds to me like he saw it coming."

"That is some big obligation, and I don't know if I could do it. But you say you knew Emma before and that you already had feelings for her, so that could probably make the situation a little easier," said Walt.

"Back to the situation with Mr. Jennings. Were you going to want me to go out there with you?" asked Walt.

"No," said Brody. "It would just be me and the marshal. I need you to stay here in town and look after things here."

"Well," said Walt, "If it's okay with you, I would like to see if I could get an advance on my pay. I need to buy some things and look for a place to stay."

"I'll give you a few dollars," said Brody. "You can go to the mercantile and get what you need. Show them your badge and just charge it to the office. I'll talk to Emma about you staying with us until you can get situated."

"Sounds like a plan," said Walt.

"You go do what you're going to do," said Brody. "I'll meet you back here for supper. I'll get Emma to fix up something for us to eat. I'll need you to stay here tonight with the prisoner. That will give me some time to talk to Emma about you staying with us."

Walt got up, thanked Brody for the job, and walked out. Brody sat at his desk, thinking for a while. He was thinking about Walt and how he reminded himself of his younger days. After a while, he got up and walked out. He mounted his horse to ride home.

When he walked into the house, he told Emma how he had hired Walt and the reasons for needing his help. He asked Emma if she would pack up some dinner for him and Walt to eat back at the jail. As he packed everything up and turned to leave, he told Emma that he had to talk to her soon and ask a favor. He walked out, got on his horse, and rode away. Emma was left wondering what in the world Brody had on his mind and what kind of favor he wanted.

Walt was at the jail when Brody got back to town. Brody got off his horse in front of the jailhouse and took all the supper fixings from Emma in with him. He placed them on the desk just as Walt was walking back in from checking on the prisoner.

"That sure smells good!" said Walt.

"Fried chicken and all the fixings," said Brody. "Help yourself. Did you manage to get everything you needed at the mercantile?"

"Mostly," said Walt. "There are a couple of things I needed that I just couldn't find."

"Well, tell the clerk what they are and maybe he can order them for you," said Brody.

When they finished supper, Brody invited Walt to go get a beer with him at the saloon. "I want to talk to you and get to know you a little bit better," said Brody.

So, they both walked into the saloon and sat down at a table. There was a new saloon girl working, and she quickly noticed them walking in. She came over and introduced herself.

"Howdy there, cowboys," she said. "My name is Becky. If y'all don't mind, I'll sit here and drink with y'all. What will it be? I'll go get it for you."

"We're just having some beers," said Brody. "But if you don't mind, we would like some time alone. We have a lot to talk about, and you might be a distraction. Next time, old Walt here can buy you a beer and spend some time with you."

Becky shook her head and left to get their beers. Brody started off asking Walt where he was from.

"I'm from a little town just outside of Topeka, Kansas," said Walt. "I was on my way down to Mexico. I've heard a lot of stories about Mexico, and I wanted to see if they were true. I was just passing through when all that ruckus at this saloon started."

"Well, I guess it was lucky for me that you were here," said Brody. "If the new marshal wants you to stay, are you going to consider it?"

"I think I might give it a try. Like I said, I've always been interested in the law," said Walt.

Becky came around with their beers. She put them down in front of them and turned to leave. But before she left, she gave Walt a thorough looking-over.

"I think she might be sweet on you," said Brody.

"Well," said Walt, "She is kind of soft on the eyes. I wouldn't mind giving her a try."

"Back to business," said Brody. "How about that trip to Mexico? You still thinking about going?"

"Well," said Walt, "That kind of depends on whether that new marshal wants to keep me on or not. I'll just wait and decide after whatever happens, happens. I'm in no hurry to go anywhere."

They sat there talking for hours. Then Brody told Walt, "Well, it's late and you need to get back to your prisoner. I'm going home to bed. I'll talk to Emma in the morning and let you know what we decide."

They both got up and walked back to the jail. Walt went in to check on the prisoner while Brody waited. He walked back out and told Brody everything was fine. Brody said his goodnights and left.

When Brody got back to the house, he put his horse up and walked inside. He looked in on Emma, but she was already fast asleep. Although he thought about going out to the barn, he decided to sleep in the extra room. He knew Emma would hog-tie him if he didn't.

In the morning, Brody was up before the sun. Emma was still asleep, so he made a pot of coffee and sat at the table to think things out. While sitting there, he heard Emma starting to stir. He got up from his seat and grabbed an extra cup for her coffee. He sat there, thinking and drinking his coffee, still waiting for Emma to come in.

She finally opened the door to the bedroom and noticed Brody sitting at the table. She walked in and said, "Good morning. I thought for sure you'd be out in the barn."

"I thought about it," said Brody, "But I knew that you would hog-tie me if you found me out there."

"You got that right," said Emma.

"Coffee's hot," said Brody. "Also, I need to talk to you regarding Walt."

"Who is Walt?" said Emma. "Oh, I remember. He's your new deputy. What about him?"

"Well," said Brody, "Seems like he was just passing through with no intention of staying around when all that went down at the saloon the other night. He has no money and no place to bunk down. This being your house and all, I thought I'd ask you if he could stay here with us until he gets situated."

"That's fine," said Emma. "We don't have any room here in the house, but he could fix up that room out there in the barn. He can stay as long as he wants. He'll be good company."

"Well," said Brody, "That was easier than I thought it would be. Would you like some breakfast?"

"I need to go to town to check on things at the jail," said Brody, "But I sure could eat. If you don't mind fixing something for Walt, too, I'll just take it with me."

"I don't mind," said Emma.

"While you're doing that," said Brody, "I'm going to go saddle up my horse and get ready for the day."

When he had everything ready to go and was prepared to leave, he went back into the house.

Emma had their breakfast ready, and Brody thanked her, said goodbye, and left. When he got back to town, he found Walt sitting outside the jail. As Brody rode up to the jail, he got off his horse and tied him up.

"Enjoying the morning?" remarked Brody to Walt.

"I sure am," said Walt. "I got tired of just lying there. I couldn't sleep anymore, so I came out here."

"How's the prisoner?" asked Brody.

"He's fine," stated Walt.

"Come on in," said Brody. "I got breakfast for you."

They both walked into the jail and sat down to eat. After breakfast, Brody told Walt to release the prisoner.

"I think he's been in there long enough," said Brody. "He's had time to think on things."

So, they let the prisoner go shortly after breakfast and sat there talking for a while. Walt wanted to know more about Emma.

"How long have you known Emma?" he asked.

"Oh, I don't know," said Brody. "I guess it's been over 20 or 25 years since I've known her. Me and Roy grew up together, but we also worked together as well for many years. Roy's the one that met Emma first. They met at a dance in the little town where we lived. I didn't meet Emma until the next day when she and Roy were eating breakfast. She seemed to be really nice, and we got to be good friends pretty fast. I even took her to a couple of dances myself. We got close, but she told me that she already had feelings for Roy. So, I told her I understood, and that Roy was just like a brother to me, and I wouldn't meddle in their love affair. After that, work took me away for a spell, and I didn't see them for a while. Then one day, out of the blue, I got a telegram saying that they were getting married and that they wanted me to be the best man. I replied, saying I would accept and promised to be there. And two weeks later, they were married and that was that. I left to go back to work, and I didn't see Roy again till I met back up with him and we chased those Irish brothers together."

"So, how in the world did Roy come to ask you to do a favor like that for him, taking care of his wife if he died?" asked Walt.

"Well," said Brody, "I guess it was like you said—he saw it coming. I noticed he was acting strange, but I really didn't think anything about it, and when he asked me, it threw me back some. I guess he always knew that I had feelings for Emma. Well, enough of that. Let's go get us some beers and see what Becky's up to."

They both got up and made their way to the saloon. As soon as they walked in, Becky saw them and went to greet them.

"Bring us a couple of beers and come sit with us," said Walt.

Becky brought the beer, sat them down, and sat next to Walt.

"Y'all having a good day?" asked Becky.

"We're having a great day," answered Brody. "It's all nice and quiet, the way I like it. Are you having a great day too, Walt?" asked Becky.

"I reckon so," answered Walt. "I just stopped in for a drink and landed a job. The company's not too bad either!"

Becky just smiled.

"Now I need to find me a place to lay my head," said Walt.

"Oh, I forgot to tell you, "said Brody. "I did talk to Emma. She said you were welcome to stay with us. There's no room in the house right now, but there's a room in the barn that you can fix up. She said that you could stay there as long as you wanted."

"Well, things are looking up for me," said Walt.

"Maybe I could come out and help fix that room up too," said Becky.

"I sure would like that," said Walt. "I'll let you know when I'm ready. For now, I'm just going to bunk down on the floor."

"Well," said Brody, "I think we had better head out. I want to take you around so you can get acquainted with the town."

Walt turned to Becky and asked, "May I call you later?"

"That would be just fine," answered Becky.

The two men got up and walked out of the saloon and started down the street.

"To tell you the truth, Walt," said Brody, "I'm going to be learning about this town, too. I haven't been here very long, and I already explained how I came into this job."

"Well," said Walt, "we'll learn this together."

As they walked through the town, they went into each establishment to introduce themselves. The townspeople were all very friendly, and they were happy to see some law enforcement in their town.

"It's getting to be late," said Brody. "I think I'm going to go home. Since you don't have a place just yet, can you stay at the jail and keep an eye on things here?"

"Sounds fine," said Walt. "When you get home, will you please thank Emma for me?"

Brody nodded his head and headed out. When he got to the house, Emma was just walking out of the front door.

"I was just about to start supper," said Emma.

"Well, while you're doing that, I'll put my horse away and then come in and help you," said Brody.

"Maybe we can talk some more when you get in?" asked Emma.

Brody just smiled and walked away. He got done with his horse and walked back into the house. Emma was at the stove cooking, so Brody started setting the table.

Brody and Emma sat down at the table to eat. Not much conversation happened during dinner. After they had finished eating, Emma started to speak. "Did Walt like the idea of moving into the barn?" asked Emma.

"Yes," said Brody. "He was really excited about the idea, and he told me to be sure and thank you. He met this saloon girl named Becky. She's going to come over and help him fix up the place."

"When is all this going to happen?" asked Emma.

"Probably starting tomorrow, I suppose," answered Brody.

"Well," said Emma, "I have some things in here that he can use to make that room a little more comfortable. Tell him, when he and Becky come out to start setting everything up, he should come in here and see me first."

"I'll let him know," said Brody. "I'm sure he'll appreciate that."

"Now, who is this Becky girl you said he met?" asked Emma. "You think there's something there?"

Brody and Emma sat down at the table to eat. Not much conversation happened during dinner. But after they had finished eating, Emma started to speak. "Did Walt like the idea of moving into my barn?" asked Emma.

"Yes," said Brody. "He was really excited about the idea, and he told me to be sure and thank you. He met this saloon girl named Becky. She's going to come over and help him fix up the place."

"When is all this going to happen?" asked Emma.

"Probably starting tomorrow, I suppose," answered Brody.

"Well," said Emma, "I have some things in here that he can use to make that room a little more comfortable. Tell him, when he and Becky come out to start setting everything up, he should come in here and see me first."

"I'll let him know," said Brody. "I'm sure he'll appreciate that."

"Now, what is this Becky girl you said he met?" asked Emma. "You think there's something there?"

"Well," said Brody, "by the way Walt looks at that girl and the way she looks at him, I would say there was something there."

"Good enough," said Emma. "When he gets settled in, we will have to have her over sometime, so that I can get to know her better. If she's going to be coming over here to see him, I'd like to know a little more about her."

"I'll let him know," said Brody. "I think I'll go and check things outside before I turn in."

"All right, well, I'm going to bed," said Emma. "Good night."

"Good night," said Brody as she turned to leave.

Outside, it was a dark, starlit night. Brody stopped at the corral and lit a cigarette. He had too much on his mind to think that he could go inside and just go to sleep. He stood there and smoked his cigarette, looking off into the darkness. He wondered what this new Marshal would be like. He had heard his name and knew that he had quite a reputation. In one more week, he would find out all he needed to know about this guy.

He heard a coyote howling off in the distance and came back to himself. He decided that he had better go in and try to get some sleep. He got ready for bed and went to lie down. He was asleep before his head hit the pillow.

In the morning, Emma stuck her head in the doorway and called his name. Brody was up in a flash.

"Good morning," said Emma. "It's getting to be late, and breakfast is already on the table."

"I guess I was more tired than I thought," said Brody.

"Walt's going to be wondering where you are!" exclaimed Emma. "I made some breakfast for both of y'all, so you can take it with you when you go."

She left the room, and he got up and got dressed. When he was ready, he grabbed the breakfast basket. Then he thanked Emma and left.

When he got to town, Walt and Becky were sitting outside the jailhouse talking. As Brody was getting down off his horse, Becky said hello and then scurried off.

"What was that all about?" asked Brody.

"Oh, not much," said Walt. "She was just telling me about an old boyfriend. He found out about us, and she thinks that he's going to cause trouble."

"Should I talk to this boyfriend?" asked Brody.

"Don't bother yourself on that," said Walt. "If he comes around here, I'll take care of it."

"Peacefully, I hope," said Brody.

"Well, that's up to the boyfriend," said Walt.

"I brought breakfast," said Brody. "Let's go on in and have some."

Walt got up and followed Brody into the jailhouse.

"Emma keeps feeding us like this, and I'm not going to be wanting to leave," said Walt.

"I know what you mean," answered Brody.

After they were done, they sat there in silence for a while.

"When do you think you and Becky will be fixing up that room?" asked Brody.

"I was thinking maybe we could go out there tomorrow and get started," said Walt.

"Good," said Brody. "But before you get started on that, you might want to go in and see Emma. She has some things she wants to give you. Also, she wants to meet your Becky. She said that she wants to get to know her if she's going to be coming over there to her place. You know how womenfolk are."

"Yeah, I reckon I do," said Walt.

"Speaking of Becky, I think I'm going to go on over and have me a beer and let her know our plan."

Walt left, and Brody started looking over some papers on the desk that had been neglected. He came across a wanted poster of a man that looked very familiar. He thought he knew the man but could not remember from where.

"It will come to me," he thought to himself.

He found another letter marked "important." He opened it and started reading. When he finished, he just sat there, dumbfounded.

"If this just don't beat all," he told himself. "I'd better go let Walt know of this situation."

He headed towards the saloon and as he was nearing the door to enter, a man came flying out and landed hard on the saloon's porch with a thud, just as Walt walked out right behind him.

"This the boyfriend?" asked Brody.

"That's right," answered Walt.

"I'll go lock him up for now," said Brody. "We need to talk about this."

"I'll be right here when you come back," answered Walt. "We can drink us some beers while we talk."

Brody was gone for a while, and in the meantime, Walt was telling Becky all about the plans and how Emma wanted to meet her. Becky started asking Walt questions about Emma. She wanted to know a little more about Emma, too, before she met her.

Walt told her not to worry.

“Y’all are gonna be good friends before you know it,” he told her.

Brody finally made it back, and they sat down to have their talk.

“I found a letter marked ‘important,’” said Brody. “It was from that new marshal. Seems like something came up, and he can’t make it for another month. Looks like you’re stuck with me till then.”

“Good,” said Walt. “That will give me a little more time to ease into this job. I wanted to work with you a little more anyway.”

“Well, don’t get too comfortable,” said Brody. “Just remember, it will be up to the marshal if he wants to keep you on as his deputy.”

"I know, I know," said Walt. "I think this will be my job, though. I can just feel it."

"Now, what about that boyfriend?" asked Brody.

"Let's go have a talk with him," said Walt. "See if he's going to behave, or if I'm gonna have to kill him."

Walt kissed Becky goodbye, and they walked out of the saloon. As they were crossing the street, the door to the jailhouse flew open, and a couple of hombres came running out. They already had their guns out, so they started shooting at the lawmen.

Before they knew it, Walt was hit in the leg and fell to the ground. Brody flipped over and came up shooting. He managed to get shots off at both the boyfriend and the unknown hombre. Both men lay dead in the street. The third hombre, who jumped on his horse to leave as quickly as possible, was not able to escape Brody's sharp shooting skills, and fell off his horse dead as Brody fired a final shot.

During all of this, Becky came running out of the saloon, crying. She ran over to Walt as he lay bleeding.

"I'm okay," said Walt. "Go check on Brody. And then, go fetch the doctor."

As Becky was leaving, Brody walked up to Walt.

"Well," he said, "I guess we don't have to worry about the boyfriend anymore. You going to make it?"

"Yeah, I'm going to be just fine," said Walt. "I won't be able to do much for a while, though."

"That's okay," said Brody. "As long as you get better."

It was midday by then, and Brody told the doctor that he wanted to talk to him. They went into another room, and Brody asked, "Do you think Walt could stay here overnight?"

"He's going to be staying over at Emma's place, but we don't have it set up quite yet."

The doctor said that would be no problem because he wanted to keep an eye on him anyway. He stepped back into the room where Walt was and told him the revised plan.

"I'll take Becky out to Emma's, so she can start fixing up your room," said Brody. "You should be able to move in there by tomorrow."

"Thank you kindly," said Walt.

"You can lay around out there until you're able to move around," joked Brody.

He and Becky said goodbye and walked out together.

"I would like to get some supplies to take over there," said Becky.

"You go ahead and do that," said Brody. "I have some things to do as well. I'll meet you back here in about an hour."

An hour later, Brody came riding up in a wagon and stopped in front of the mercantile. Becky came walking out with two men behind her, carrying all sorts of supplies. They put everything in the wagon, and Becky hopped in. They left.

When they got to the ranch, Emma was standing on the porch waiting for them.

"Did y'all buy the store out?" Emma laughed.

"Well, it's just things I think Walt will need," answered Becky.

They both got out of the wagon, and Brody introduced Becky to Emma. They talked for a little while, and then Emma reminded Becky that she had better start unloading the wagon.

Emma took Becky into the barn to show her the room, while Brody began unloading the wagon.

"We can fix this up nice," said Becky.

"When will Walt be moving out here?" asked Emma.

"The doctor said he would be ready by tomorrow," answered Becky.

"Do you have a place, or will you be staying out here as well?" asked Emma.

"I have my own place in town," answered Becky. "I would like to spend a little time out here with Walt, though, if it's okay."

"That would be fine," said Emma.

It was late when they got done, so Emma headed inside to start supper. Becky followed right behind her. Brody went and sat on the corral, pondering the situation. He was thinking about the man on the wanted poster.

After a minute, it hit him like a lightning bolt. The man in the Wanted picture was the same man that Roy had knocked out for cheating at cards! It seemed that someone had caught him cheating again, and this time, he had killed the accuser.

"I'll remember that face," Brody thought to himself, as Emma came out to tell Brody that supper was ready. They both walked into the house together. They had a nice, quiet evening, and when supper was over, Brody went back outside to smoke a cigarette and do some more thinking.

After a while, Becky came wandering out to sit beside Brody.

"I'm sorry we had to kill that fellow of yours," said Brody.

"He was no good," answered Becky. "If y'all hadn't done it, somebody else would have."

"I was talking to Emma, and she gave me the impression that she thought I was going to move in out here with Walt."

"I don't know where she might have gotten that idea," answered Brody.

"I think I'm going to turn in," said Brody.

Becky stayed out there long after Brody had gone in. She sat there for what seemed like an eternity, just thinking. Finally, Emma came out to talk to her.

"You know, it's getting late," she said. "You might as well stay in Walt's room tonight. See how it feels."

Becky agreed and left then to do just that. She lay down on the bed but could not sleep. She had too much on her mind, especially thinking about what Emma had said. The night was long, and Becky finally fell asleep. She had just closed her eyes, it seemed, before opening them and discovering that morning had come.

A little while later, Emma came out to see if she was ready for breakfast.

Becky asked her to please sit down. Their conversation from the previous evening had been weighing on her mind.

"Did I misunderstand, or did you hint to the fact that I should move out here with Walt?" Becky asked Emma.

"I was just thinking," said Emma, "it would sure be nice to have someone else out here with me. With Brody coming and going, and Walt also being in and out, it would be great to have someone steady here with me, especially another woman that I can talk to."

"I don't know how Walt would feel about that," said Becky. "We haven't really even sat down and talked about any of this."

"How about," said Emma, "we make a big meal on Sunday, and we can all talk about the next things that may happen out here?"

"Brody has told me he'll be leaving here in the next couple of weeks and that will leave Walt here alone, and he will need to spend a lot of time in town."

The two ladies walked into the house and found Brody already sitting at the dining table.

"What have you two been up to?" asked Brody.

"We have been talking," answered Emma. "We're planning a big dinner here on Sunday. We have something that we need to talk to you and Walt about."

"Oh, I don't like the sound of this," said Brody.

After breakfast, Brody told Becky, "I'll take you back to town."

The ride back to town was silent. When they got to town, Walt was at the jailhouse waiting for them.

"What are you doing down here?" asked Brody.

"I couldn't stand it anymore," said Walt. "I had Doc rig me up these walking sticks."

Brody said, "You'll be going out to the ranch today anyway. These ladies have fixed up your room right nice."

Becky told Walt, "We need to talk."

"I'll leave y'all to it," said Brody. "I'm going to walk around town and check on things."

After Brody left, Becky sat Walt down and started explaining things to him.

"We can talk about it again on Sunday, at the gathering Emma and I have planned. I'm going on over to my place now because I have some things I need to take care of."

"Wait," said Walt. "What do I do?"

"You're on your own for now," said Becky.

She gave Walt a kiss on the forehead and left.

An hour later, Brody came walking in.

"Did Becky tell you about the big gathering?" asked Brody.

"Yeah," said Walt. "What's that all about?"

"I don't know," said Brody. "They have something up their sleeves. And I don't know if I'm going to like it."

Brody sat down at his desk. He found that Wanted poster on the guy that Roy had fought. He showed it to Walt.

"His name is Lester, Les Higgins. He's wanted for murder. My partner Roy and him had it out over a card game a while back. He's a snake. Keep your eyes open for this one. But don't try to take him yourself. He's mine. I want him."

"You want to go have a couple of beers before I take you out to the place?" Brody asked.

"Sounds good," said Walt.

The two men were sitting at the saloon, drinking a beer, when a lady and a couple of bad-looking hombres walked in. Brody looked up.

“Linda, what are you doing here?” asked Brody.

Linda walked over to where they were sitting.

“I heard you were watching over things this way,” said Linda. “I came because my father is getting tired of waiting for the railroad people. I'm afraid he might do something drastic.”

“I'm very sorry,” said Brody. “I should have sent word to you. I got a telegram from the government saying to stay put. They're sending in a new marshal, but he's not due in for another week or two. They want me to brief him on the situation before we go out there to talk to your father.

This is Walt. I just hired him as my new deputy, and we've been holding the fort down until the marshal gets here.”

“You know,” said Linda, “that's all fine and well, but my family was left not knowing anything. My father's fit to be tied!”

"Again," Brody said, "I'm very sorry. I got busy here and haven't had time to think about y'all's situation out there. Tell your dad not to lose his head over this, and we'll be out there in another week or two."

One of the men that had come with Linda took a step towards Brody.

"Not now," said Linda.

"Good advice," said Brody as he stood up. He hugged Linda and told her to go on home and tell her father about the new developments.

After they left, Brody told Walt that they should head over to the ranch.

"For a second," said Walt, "I thought I was going to see you in action."

"What's that?" said Brody. "That was just a young punk too eager to die."

They both got up and walked back to the jailhouse. Walt sat down while Brody was at his desk looking over paperwork. When he was done, he told Walt that he would go over to the livery stable to secure a buckboard for the trip out to Emma's place.

Brody pulled the buckboard up to the door of the jailhouse. He walked in and told Walt that everything was ready. Walt hobbled out to the buckboard and got into it.

Just then, Becky came walking up.

"Looks like y'all have everything taken care of," she said. "I will come out tonight if that's alright."

"That's fine," said Walt.

Walt gave Becky a kiss, and they left.

Emma was already waiting for them when they came, pulling up the driveway.

"How peaceful of a ride was that?" joked Emma, as she nodded her head toward the rear of the buckboard. Walt had fallen fast asleep.

"I don't know how he could have fallen asleep through all of that," commented Brody.

They woke him up then, laughing as they got him out of the buckboard and to his new room.

"Y'all did a nice, right job on this room," exclaimed Walt.

"That was all Becky," said Emma. "She wanted you to be comfortable."

"Well," said Walt, "I'm thankful that she'll be coming out tonight. If she wants, would it be okay if she spent the night? I wouldn't want her going back into town by herself after what has been happening lately."

"That would be fine," said Emma. "We'll leave you now so that you can go back to sleep."

Brody and Emma walked out of the room and into the house. As they were sitting at the kitchen table, Brody started telling her what had happened in town with Linda.

"Sounds like an uneasy situation," said Emma.

"Sure is," said Brody. "We need to get out there fast. I'm going back into town to send the railroad people a telegram. They need to be ready to move."

"I have a few things outside I need to do," said Emma, "and then I'm going to come in and start getting our supper ready. When you come back to the house, would you bring Becky with you?

Brody left for town and headed straight for the telegraph office. When he was done there, he went by the jailhouse. Becky was waiting there for him. She immediately asked Brody if Walt liked his new room.

"He was very happy," answered Brody. "Let me check the mail, and then we'll head on out. I left the buckboard at the library stable already. Did you get everything you need?" Brody asked her.

"Yes, I did," said Becky. "I'm anxious to get out there and see Walt in his new room."

Brody finished looking at the mail, got up, and told Becky he would bring the buckboard around. When they got over to the house, Emma heard them and went out to greet them.

"Any noise from Walt's room?" asked Brody.

"Not a peep," said Emma. "He must still be sleeping. Y'all come on in and let him sleep a little bit longer. Supper's ready. We can go ahead and eat. And Becky can take Walt a plate to go."

Here is the text with punctuation added:

After dinner, Brody told Becky, "Go on, go check on your man. I'm gonna put the horses and the buckboard away, and I'll be in after that."

"Okay," said Becky. She fixed up a plate for Walt and took it to his room. When she got there, he was fast asleep. Becky decided to wake him up.

As he stirred, he groggily said, "I didn't know I was so tired. I can't seem to keep my eyes open."

"Sleep is good for you," said Becky. "It will help you heal faster. I brought you supper."

"I'm hungry," said Walt. "I could eat a horse."

"Well, it's not a horse, but this should fill you up," said Becky. Walt proceeded to eat his supper while Becky put things away and tidied up the room.

"I talked to Emma," said Walt. "She said it would be all right for you to stay here for the night."

"Okay," said Becky, "but I won't stay here in this room with you. I'll see if she has anything in the house." A few minutes later, Emma and Brody had come up with a suitable plan.

“I talked with Brody,” Emma told Becky. “You can sleep in his room, and Brody’s going to bunk with Walt.”

“I’d hate to put Brody out!” said Becky.

“It was Brody’s idea,” said Emma. “He thought it might be too early in the relationship for y’all to sleep in the same room.”

“Well, he’s right,” said Becky. “I love Walt, but I still don’t feel comfortable enough to do that.

“Well, I think I’ll go on to bed,” said Becky.

Morning came very early. Emma was in the kitchen, fixing breakfast when Becky walked in. The sun was still down, but Becky wanted to check on Walt.

“Do you think the boys are up?” asked Becky.

“I don’t know about Walt, but Brody is already gone,” said Emma. “I heard him ride out a little earlier.”

“I’m going to go and check on Walt now,” said Becky.

As she walked out of the house, she noticed a light on in the room. Walt was in bed, but awake when Becky knocked on the door.

"Come on in," said Walt.

Becky walked in and went to sit on the side of Walt's bed.

"How did you sleep?" she asked him.

"Like a bear," said Walt. "I woke up when I heard Brody stirring around. I guess he went into town to check on things."

"Emma's fixing breakfast for you," said Becky. "Would you like me to bring you some?"

"How about just some coffee?" said Walt. "I have been meaning to sit down and talk with you."

"Okay, give me a second. I'll be right back," said Becky.

She came back with the coffee a few minutes later.

"You wanted to talk to me?" asked Becky.

"I want you to listen to me, to sit down and really listen to this," said Walt. "I have been thinking on it, and I'm pretty sure you know how I feel about you. And nothing would make me happier than to settle down with someone just like yous. When the new marshal gets here, he may not want to keep me on as deputy, and that has me worried. If he keeps me on, everything will be fine. But if he decides he wants someone else, I don't know that I'm going to want to stick around this town. Where will that leave us? If I decide to leave, are you going to want to go with me? I can't ask you to leave everything behind. You have everything here."

"I know there are a lot of questions," said Becky. "I think you're putting the cart before the horse, though. Let's just wait and see. There's no point in worrying about that now."

"Brody says the new marshal will be here within the next week or so. Then they will be leaving to go to the Jennings place, and he will need me to stay until they get back. I think we have time to think things out."

Meanwhile in town, Brody was catching up on the mail. He decided that he would take a walk through the town and check on things. As he was doing that, a stagecoach pulled into town. He stopped to see who would be getting off. A pretty lady with a little boy got off and saw Brody. Immediately, she noticed his badge. She went directly up to him and introduced herself.

"Hello," she said. "My name is Mrs. Robertson, Hilda Robertson. I'm the marshal's wife, and this is Peter, our son. Cody sent us on ahead to get settled in while he tied up some loose ends."

"It's nice to meet y'all," said Brody. "My name is Brody, Brody Thompson. How far behind y'all? Did you say he was?"

"Not too far," said Hilda. "Maybe a couple of days. He knows how urgent the situation is over here, but he had to tie up some other things where we came from. Can you tell me where we might find a room? I'm anxious to get settled in."

"I understand," said Brody. "Y'all must be tired from the ride. Y'all are going to be staying at the Roadhouse Inn. It's the nicest accommodations in town. Everything has been taken care of already. It has a dining room if you're hungry, and I will get someone to take your luggage to your room."

"We could sure eat a bite," said Hilda. "Would you come sit with us? I have a few questions I would like to ask."

"Yes, ma'am," said Brody, as they made their way to the hotel. They walked in and sat at a table near the door.

"What's on your mind?" asked Brody.

"I would like to know more about this town," said Linda

"Is there a school where Peter can attend classes? What do people do around here? That sort of thing," asked Hilda.

"Well," said Brody, "first, there is no school. There aren't very many children in these parts just yet. There are a couple of big ranches, and people just work on their own land. I hired a young man as my deputy, and I'm hoping the marshal will want to keep him on. You're going to get to meet him later today when I take you out to meet Emma. Emma is the wife of the man who was the former marshal. The young man is out of sorts right now. He got shot in the leg and is recuperating at Emma's house. He shouldn't be down and out for too much longer.

"Well, I'm going to leave you now so that you can get settled. I'll come for you in the morning, and we can go out to Emma's place. Don't eat breakfast here at the hotel—Emma will want to feed y'all!"

Hilda just smiled as Brody got up and left.

Brody finished his walk through town and went back to the jail. He opened the door to find Becky waiting for him.

"Becky, how did you get here?" Brody asked.

"I know my way around a horse," said Becky. "I hitched up the buckboard and came on in. Just so you know, Walt is talking crazy. He's already talking about leaving. He doesn't think the new marshal is going to want to keep him on."

"Well, that's just crazy talk," said Brody. "It wouldn't be very smart for the marshal not to keep him on—him already being in this position."

"I know," said Becky. "He's got it in his head that the marshal isn't going to want him, and he's making plans to leave the town."

"I'll talk to him," said Brody.

"I appreciate that!" said Becky. "Oh, and Brody, I left the buckboard at the livery stable."

Just then, Becky left to go to the Roadhouse Inn to meet the new marshal's wife. Brody went to the stable to check on the buckboard and to tell the stable boy that he would need it again in the morning and to have it ready.

Becky walked into the Roadhouse Inn and saw Hilda and her son sitting there.

"Hello," said Becky. "My name is Becky, Becky Potter. You must be the new marshal's wife."

"Yes, I am," said Hilda. "My name is Hilda Robertson, and this is my son Peter."

"It's nice to meet you," said Becky. "I hope I am not out of line here, but Brody Thompson, the Texas Ranger that you met with earlier, suggested I should come and talk to you about the marshal keeping the new deputy on. His name is Walt, and I am his new girlfriend. I wouldn't ordinarily do something like this, but Walt has been talking about leaving the town if the new marshal doesn't keep him on, and I really don't want that to happen!"

"My husband is a fair man," said Hilda. "I'm sure he will want to keep Walt on, especially with Brody's recommendation. Now, if you would excuse us, we would like to go up to our room and get settled in. We can talk more about this later."

"That would be so nice," said Becky, and with that, she left the inn. She planned to go out to Emma's in the morning with Brody. For tonight, she would stay in her old room here in town and get some much-needed rest.

Just then, she heard a knock at her door.

"Who is it?" she asked.

"It's me, Brody," said the voice from the other side.

She opened the door and found Brody standing there.

"I just wanted to let you know that Hilda and the boy are going to go out to Emma's with me first thing in the morning. Would you like to go with us?"

"Yes," said Becky. "If that's okay, I would really like to talk to Mrs. Robertson some more about Walt."

"We're planning to leave here around six," said Brody.

Morning came early, but Becky was ready. She went down to the sheriff's office. She noticed the buckboard out in front, but Brody was nowhere to be found. She figured he must have gone after Hilda and decided to wait inside. After a little while, she heard them coming down the walk and went outside to greet them. They exchanged pleasantries, got on the buckboard, and left.

The sun was peeking over the horizon when they got to the ranch. Emma had heard them coming and was outside waiting to greet them. Brody got down from his horse and started helping the women down. The little boy just jumped off.

"This is Hilda Robertson," said Brody.

Emma stepped up and gave Hilda a hug. Hilda offered Emma her condolences, and they all walked inside.

"Breakfast will be ready in just a moment," said Emma. "If y'all would like to just sit down, I'll bring it to you."

As Emma walked into the kitchen, Becky was right behind her.

"I thought you would have spent the night last night," said Emma.

"I didn't want to wear out my welcome," said Becky.

"That will never happen," said Emma.

They enjoyed a lovely breakfast cooked by Emma. Immediately following breakfast, Becky once again began talking to Hilda again about the marshal keeping Walt on as deputy.

"Just like I said," interjected Hilda, "I don't see a problem with Cody keeping Walt on as deputy, not with Brody's recommendation. And I would sure like to meet this young man. He must be a pretty important guy. Is he available?"

"Let me go see if he's awake," said Becky.

Walt was just putting his boots on when Becky knocked on the door.

"Come on in," said Walt.

Becky opened the door and told him, "Good morning. Are you ready for your breakfast? The new marshal's wife is here, and she wants to meet you. I may have been talking about you with her," Becky smiled.

"Is that right?" said Walt. "What have you been saying to this woman?"

"I've been telling her it wouldn't be smart for the new marshal not to keep you on as his deputy," said Becky.

"Well, that could be true," said Walt. "You sure do beat all! I've never met a woman quite like you."

"Is that a good thing or a bad thing?" asked Becky shyly.

"Well, I guess that's a good thing!" answered Walt.

The two got up and headed to the house. When they walked in, everyone was in the kitchen. Walt went up to Hilda and introduced himself right away.

“Well,” said Hilda, “I can already see that you're a fine young man. I don't think Cody's going to have any problem keeping you on as deputy. Becky here has really been talking you up.”

“Oh, yeah,” said Walt. “She's really something.”

Hilda said, “You must be hungry. Why don't you sit down and have a bite to eat? We'll talk some more after you're finished.”

Hilda got up and headed outside. Everyone else followed her.

“This sure is a beautiful place Emma has,” said Hilda. “I hope that Cody and I can have something like this one day.”

“It sure is,” said Brody. “Roy knew a lot about the land. There was nothing here when he bought it.”

“I think that's why I loved him so much,” said Emma. “He had a good eye for things like that.”

"Roy was one of a kind," said Brody. "I was sure proud to call him a friend."

"Well, I sure hope we can settle down and become a part of this community," said Hilda. "It seems to be so nice and peaceful here."

Brody said, "I hate to leave good company, but I really need to get back to town and get things ready for when our new marshal gets here. Please tell Walt just to keep taking it easy."

Brody got on his horse and rode off.

"So," Hilda said to Emma, "what's the story between you two, if it's not too personal for me to ask?"

"Well," said Emma, "it is a long story. But if you have time, here goes. Brody has known my Roy for a long time. They grew up together. I actually met Brody first, and we hit it off. We saw each other from time to time. Brody was gone a lot of the time, him being a ranger and all.

"One day, right after Roy became marshal, Brody introduced him to me. With him being around more than Brody, we started seeing each other. Brody's and my relationship never quite took off. And then one day, out of the blue, Roy up and proposed to me.

"I told him that I would want to talk to Brody before I could give him an answer. The next time Brody was in town, we talked, and I told him. And then he told me that he could not be any happier for us. He told us that with Roy being more stable, it would be a great fit."

The next day, I told Roy that I would be honored to accept his invitation to be his wife. We made our preparations, and Roy asked Brody to be his best man.

When Roy left to go help Brody with those bank robbers, I just had a funny feeling about that entire situation. When I saw Brody riding alone and noticed he had Roy's horse, all of my fears were realized. I lost it.

The next day, Brody and I sat down and talked about everything. He explained what had happened and about the promise he had made to Roy.

"What type of promise was that?" Hilda asked.

"I guess Roy knew something was going to happen," said Emma. "He made Brody promise him that if something were to happen to him, he would take me on as his wife and take care of me as long as I needed."

"That sure was thoughtful of Roy and nice of Brody to make those arrangements," said Hilda.

"Roy knew that Brody and I had been close," said Emma.

"That couldn't have been easy for Roy," said Hilda.

The next day, Brody and I made a promise that we would wait to see how things went before we made any more decisions.

"Well, where do Becky and Walt fit into this picture?" asked Hilda.

"Walt saved Brody's life one day in a fight in the saloon!" said Emma. "Brody has said that Walt reminds him of a younger version of himself, and he hired him as deputy and took him under his wing."

"One day, Brody and Walt were having some drinks in the saloon, and that's where Walt met Becky. Becky had just started working there as a waitress, and they hit it off right away. Walt has been talking a lot to Becky about leaving this town, and that's why she hopes the new marshal will agree to keep him on as deputy."

"That's very sweet," said Hilda. "And under the circumstances, I would probably do the same thing I would talk to anybody and everybody that would listen to help keep my man close by."

"I think Walt and Becky make a great couple," said Emma. "If things work out, they will stay here with me, of course, until they can find a place of their own. I imagine that there will be a wedding in the near future."

"I love weddings!" exclaimed Hilda.

Just then, Walt and Becky came walking out of the house.

"I see what you mean," said Hilda, "about them making a great couple."

They all stood there talking for a while longer until Hilda spoke up.

"It's starting to get late," she said. "Peter and I better get back to town and get settled in for the night."

"When you're ready," said Becky, "I'll drive you back to town in the buckboard."

"Thank you," said Hilda, as they all said their goodbyes and left.

On the way back to town, Hilda reminded Becky not to worry. "I will talk to my husband about Walt."

And they rode the rest of the way back to town in silence. When they arrived, they pulled up in front of the jailhouse. To their surprise, Cody, the new marshal, came walking out to greet them.

"Cody!" said Hilda, "When did you get here?"

"Oh, about an hour ago," said Cody.

"Daddy!" said Peter, giving his father a hug.

Hilda introduced Becky to him and told him that she would explain who Becky was. "We'll talk later," she said.

"My guess is that you're probably pretty tired," said Hilda. "We have a room at the Roadhouse Inn. Let's go get you settled in."

"That would be great," said Cody. "Let me just finish things up here with Brody, and I will met you there in a little while. Hilda agreed and she and Peter left for the inn.

Becky also left and promised to return the buckboard to the stable.

Brody and Cody headed back into the jailhouse to finish discussing upcoming business. "When do you think you might be ready to go to the Jennings place?" Brody asked Cody.

"If I could have a day or two to get settled in and get my head cleared," said Cody, "then I would be ready to head that way."

He said goodbye to Brody and left. When he finally got to the inn, Hilda was waiting for him in the lobby.

"Are you hungry, dear?" asked Hilda. "I thought maybe we could go have something to eat and sit down and catch up."

"There must be something really important on your mind," said Cody.

They sat down to eat and ended up talking for hours.

"It's getting late," said Cody. "We had better get some sleep. I want to get acquainted with this town before Brody and I go out to see Mr. Jennings. I would also like to meet this young man, Walt."

Hilda said, "Cody, he is a kind, young man, and he has a girl who really cares deeply for him. Emma, the lady I mentioned earlier, and Brody think highly of him, too!"

"Sounds like he could make a good deputy," said Cody. "And it also sounds like you ladies have made up my mind for me. We will see how he does when we go to the Jennings place. I plan to tell Brody that I want Walt to go over there with us."

The next morning, Cody headed to the jailhouse. As he walked up to the jail, Cody noticed the buckboard sitting out front. He walked into the jailhouse and found Brody sitting at the desk.

"What's the buckboard for?" asked Cody.

Brody answered, "I thought we could take the womenfolk and go out to Emma's. This way you can meet Walt and see how he and Becky are together. We'll make a day of it, and you can get to know everyone."

"That sounds like a good idea," said Cody. "I think I've already been sold on him as deputy. I thought maybe it's a good idea that we take him with us when we go out to the Jennings place. I want to see how he handles himself out there."

"Good idea," said Brody. "Let's just wait on those women now, and when they're ready, we'll head out."

An hour later, Hilda, Peter, and Becky came walking up, carrying baskets. Cody was just about to say something, but Hilda cut him off.

"It's lunch," Hilda said.

The women and Peter climbed on the buckboard, and they took off. When they got to Emma's, she came outside to greet them. The two women and Peter got down off the buckboard and began unloading the baskets.

"Are we expecting an army here?" said Emma.

Hilda laughed. "Well, we brought a little of everything. Since we'll be out here all day, I don't think anything will get wasted."

Becky went to the barn to get Walt and to let him know that the new marshal had arrived. She knocked on his door, and heard him say, "Come in."

"Good morning," said Becky to Walt. "We brought you breakfast. The new marshal arrived early, and he's here with Hilda and Peter. We plan to make a day of it, and he would like to meet and get to know you."

Walt quickly finished putting his boots on, and he and Becky walked outside. Walt headed straight to Cody and introduced himself.

"It's nice to finally meet you," said Cody to Walt. "Everyone around here has been saying nothing but good things about you. I feel like I already know you. The deputy job is yours if you'd like it, although there is one challenge I have for you."

Walt responded, "Thank you so much for the opportunity. I will try to live up to your expectations. I am curious about this challenge you have for me, though."

Cody said, "I would like for you to go out to Mr. Jennings' place with Brody and me. I want to see how you handle certain situations. I've already discussed this plan with Brody, and he agrees that this will be a good test of your character. The railroad people have already been contacted and will be on the morning stage, and they will ride out there with us tomorrow."

"Sounds like you already have a great plan," said Walt.

"Well, not everything," said Cody. "We will have to spend tomorrow in town getting our plans ready and making sure that we're prepared."

For the rest of the day, everyone enjoyed themselves eating, visiting, and getting to know one another more. It started to get late, and Cody suggested that they go back to town. They said their goodbyes, and before they left, Cody told Brody and Walt, "I'll see you both in the office first thing in the morning."

They both responded with a nod of their heads, saying, "Yes, sir."

Once they left, Brody and Emma told Becky that she could spend the night if she'd like.

"You can have my room again," said Brody, "and I'll bunk in the barn with Walt. Since we'll be leaving really early in the morning, you could just stay out here and help Emma clean up, if you don't mind."

"I do like that plan," said Becky, and they all said goodnight and went to bed.

The next morning, the sun was just coming up when Brody and Walt made it to town. They pulled up in front of the jailhouse and dismounted. Cody came out of the jailhouse to greet them.

"Morning, gentlemen. Let's just start here by filling me in on this entire situation out at the Jennings place," said Cody.

"Well, it's pretty simple," said Brody. "The railroad wants to lay tracks through some of Brad's land, and he won't hear of it. He has hired some gunmen to help keep them out. He told them if they came on his land, he would bury them."

"That's some pretty serious talk," said Cody. "Has he kept his word?"

"Not yet," said Brody, "although I had to kill a couple of his guns last time when Roy and I went out there."

"How did that happen?" asked Cody.

"Well, three of them met us out on the prairie," said Brody, "and they wouldn't let us go any further and commenced to draw their guns on us. They were too slow, though."

"Let's hope that doesn't happen this time," said Cody. "They should be expecting us this time. The railroad people will be there, and they will ride out with us first thing in the morning. I sure hope Jennings will be in a listening mood this time!"

"Walt, I want you to keep alert and make sure no one gets trigger-happy. I know this is my baby, but, Brody, I want you to do most of the talking. You know more about the situation than I do. I guess that'll be all, except just to say that we all need to remember to keep our wits about us and make sure that we all come back safe.

"Let's go get us some breakfast, boys, and we'll finalize our plans," said Cody.

After breakfast, Cody headed back to the hotel, and Brody and Walt went to the Sheriff's office.

"Do you think everything is going to go as planned?" asked Walt.

"I'm not sure," said Brody. "Like Cody said, keep your eyes open for any trouble."

The rest of the day went by with them talking and making sure that their plan for tomorrow was intact. Evening came, and Cody sent word for Walt and Brody to meet him and his family at the hotel for supper.

The men enjoyed a meal together and had easy conversation. It was becoming clearer each day spent together that they were very like-minded and would do well working together.

After supper, Cody told the other men they should go home and get some rest because the next day was going to be a long one.

It was already late when they got back to the ranch. Becky was the first to see them coming up the drive.

“What are you doing here?” asked Walt.

“I’m going to stay out here with Emma while y’all are gone,” said Becky.

“That will make me feel so much better,” said Brody. “We already ate supper, and now we really need to get some shut eye.”

They all said their good nights, and the men headed to the barn. It seemed as though the night flew by.

“You up?” asked Walt.

“I never went to sleep,” said Brody.

"Me neither," said Walt. "I've got too much on my mind. I don't want to let the new marshal down."

"It'll be okay," said Brody. "We better get up and moving and get on over to the jail."

It was still dark outside when they left. When they got to the jailhouse, Brody made a pot of coffee.

"Now we'll just sit and wait," said Brody.

"What time do you expect the stage?" asked Walt.

"It should be here about 7 a.m.," said Brody. "They made a special run just for the railroad people. I think it should just be the two men, officers that are high up in the company."

After that, they sat in silence, drinking their coffee. It was 6:30 when Cody came walking in.

"Are you boys ready?" he asked.

"As ready as we can be," said Brody.

"Shouldn't be long now," Cody replied. He joined them in having a cup of coffee.

The 7 o'clock hour came and went with no stage. The men started to get a little antsy about things. At 7:45, they finally heard the sound of some horses.

"That must be them," said Cody.

The stage pulled right up to the jailhouse, and the three men went out to meet it. The stage pulled up, and the door opened. Out stepped a woman. A man got out behind her.

"I thought it was supposed to be two men," said Cody.

"It was, but Mr. Watson couldn't make it, so they sent Ms. Parsons," said the man. "My name is John Mitchell, and this is Lucy Parsons. Don't worry, Ms. Parsons is very capable of holding her own."

"That's fine with us," said Brody. "But I don't know if Mr. Jennings will take her seriously."

"Well, he's just going to have to," said Lucy. "I think we're going to be fine."

"Okay," said Brody. "We have a buggy all ready for you at the library stable if you want to follow me."

They all walked to the library stable where the buggy was waiting. The boys got on their horses, and off they went.

When they got within five miles of the Jennings place, they were met by some riders. One man spoke up and asked, "Are y'all the railroad group?"

"Yes, we are," said Brody. "I think Mr. Jennings is expecting us."

"Yep, he's been expecting y'all for some time," said the man. "Come on, we'll take y'all on in."

"Thanks. Appreciate it," said Brody. "Lead the way."

"Did you see who it is?" said Walt.

"Sure did," said Brody. "Don't let on that you know anything."

"Did I miss something?" asked Cody.

"The man that did the talking is a wanted man," Brody informed him. "We just got the wanted poster on him the other day. He's also a personal problem."

"Do you think he recognized you?" asked Walt.

"I don't think so," said Brody. "Let's go on in and deal with this situation first, and I'll take care of him later on our way out."

They got to the ranch house, and everyone got out. Linda came out to meet them. She told her ranch hands to take care of their horses, and as they walked into the house, Mr. Jennings was coming down the stairs.

"Looks like y'all finally made it," Mr. Jennings said. "Sit down, let's get this over with."

Brody introduced the railroad people, and they all sat down.

"I didn't expect to be dealing with a woman," exclaimed Brad Jennings.

"Oh, don't mind me," said Lucy. "Don't think of me as a woman and just know that I am perfectly capable of handling anything that you throw at me. I am a railroad executive, and you can treat me as such."

"Yes, ma'am," said Brad, "but I still don't know what you can say that will change my mind."

They all sat down, and Mr. Mitchell started off the conversation.

"Mr. Jennings," he said, "we have done a lot of thinking and planning. We looked at a map of your property. We found all we need from you is a little strip of your land on the west side. It will run along your property line for about five miles. We looked at it from every angle, and there is just no way around it."

"See there," Brad said. "I don't know that I want to give that up."

"Like I said," interjected Mr. Mitchell, "there is just no way around it. We are willing to pay you double what the land is worth, but we really do need it."

"Excuse me," said Brody, "I need to go out and get some air."

The men kept on talking while Brody got up and stepped outside. Linda, standing up behind her father, slipped away and headed outside behind Brody.

Outside, Brody was lighting himself a cigarette. As Linda came over to stand next to him, he said, "Your father is a hard man."

"He is just set in his ways," said Linda. "It took him a long time to build up what he has, and he lost Mama about halfway through it."

"I'm sorry," said Brody. "That must have been hard."

"What about you?" asked Linda. "What's your story? I noticed you looking my way last time. I'm a lot like my father. I don't beat around the bush. If I see something I want, I go after it. You have a few years on me, but I like that on a man. Makes me think that you know how to treat a lady."

Brody nodded and said, "I'll admit, you do look good to me, but right now I'm not in a position to do anything about it."

"What's that supposed to mean?" asked Linda.

Brody replied, "I made a promise to someone that I would look after his wife. My partner and good friend got killed, and I promised him that I would take care of her."

"That's a very admirable thing to do," said Linda. "But does that mean you have to marry her?"

"No, I reckon not," said Brody. "But it happened very recently, and I'm still thinking about what I should do next."

Linda was about to say something when Walt stepped out and informed Brody that Cody wanted him to come back in. Brody excused himself and stepped back inside. The men were finishing up.

"I'm going to have to think about it," said Brad Jennings. "Seems like you have me against a wall here. I need to sit down with my daughter and talk about it. Give me a couple of weeks to make my decision."

"Sounds reasonable," said Mr. Mitchell. "Meanwhile, we will get all the paperwork started. We really would appreciate your cooperation, Mr. Jennings."

As the men were leaving, Brody pulled Brad aside.

"I need to let you know something," Brody said. "One of the men on your payroll is a wanted man. We just got the poster on him earlier, and we are going to be taking him down."

"Which one is it?" Brad asked.

"His name is Lester, but he goes by Les. Les Higgins," answered Brody. "I just thought you should know what was happening, also so that you can keep your other men handled."

"Consider it done," said Brad. "Do what you have to do. I have no quarrel against local lawmen."

When they stepped outside, Brody pulled Walt aside.

"I plan to take Higgins down, and I need you to watch my back. I already let Mr. Jennings know what was going down, and he's going to be handling his other men."

"I'm right behind you," Walt assured him.

Mr. Jennings' men were all standing around outside, and Les was standing right in the front, talking to another man. From where they were standing, the lawmen would have to walk right by them. Brody took the lead, with Walt right behind him.

As Brody walked by Les, he drew his gun and identified himself.

"Les," he said.

Les, startled, reached for his own gun, but before he could pull it out, Brody reached out and punched him right in the face. Les fell backward, and as he did, his gun went flying.

As all this was happening, the other men began going for their guns. Walt already had his out.

"Let's all just take it easy," Walt said.

Mr. Jennings came walking up then, right behind Walt.

"All right, men," said Brad Jennings. "You heard the deputy. Everybody take it easy. Seems like Mr. Higgins is a wanted man."

By that time, Lester was just getting back on his feet.

"You have nothing on me!" Lester objected.

"That's where you're wrong," answered Brody. "We just got the wanted poster on you this morning!"

"You are wanted for murder, and it seems like you don't learn. You killed a man for accusing you of cheating at cards. You don't remember me, do you? The two men in the saloon at Sandy Fork. My friend accused you of cheating, and you probably would have killed him if I hadn't stopped you."

Lester didn't say a word.

The three lawmen and Lester got on their horses and rode off.

www.ingramcontent.com/pod-product-compliance
Lightning Source LLC
Chambersburg PA
CBHW071434300726
48976CB00004B/1328

* 9 7 8 1 9 6 5 6 7 9 9 2 0 *